The Tiara Club

VIVIAN FRENCH

The Tiara Club

Princess Charlotte

AND THE

Birthday Ball

ILLUSTRATED BY SARAH GIBB

KATHERINE TEGEN BOOKS
An Imprint of HarperCollins*Publishers*

The Tiara Club: Princess Charlotte and the Birthday Ball
Text copyright © 2007 by Vivian French
Illustrations copyright © 2007 by Sarah Gibb

Library of Congress Cataloging-in-Publication Data
French, Vivian.
Princess Charlotte and the birthday ball / Vivian French ;
illustrated by Sarah Gibb. — 1st U.S. ed.
p.   cm. — (The Tiara Club)
Summary: On her first day at the Princess Academy, Princess
Charlotte inadvertently causes an accident that ruins the dresses
of her new roommates and unless something can be done none
of them will be able to attend the much anticipated Birthday
Ball.
ISBN-10: 0-06-112431-1 (trade bdg.)
ISBN-13: 978-0-06-112431-0 (trade bdg.)
ISBN-10: 0-06-112428-1 (pbk.)
ISBN-13: 978-0-06-112428-0 (pbk.)
[1.   Princesses—Fiction. 2.   Friendship—Fiction.
3. Magic—Fiction. 4. Schools—Fiction.] I. Gibb, Sarah, ill.
II. Title.
PZ7.F88917Prac 2007   2006019225
[Fic]—dc22   CIP
                                                          AC

Typography by Amy Ryan
1 2 3 4 5 6 7 8 9 10
❖
First U.S. edition, 2007

For dearest Charlotte,
always and forever a princess,
with much love
xx
—V.F.

For my big sis,
Princess Charlotte
—S.G.

The Royal Palace Academy
for the Preparation of Perfect Princesses
(Known to our students as "The Princess Academy")

OUR SCHOOL MOTTO:
*A Perfect Princess always thinks of others before herself,
and is kind, caring, and truthful.*

We offer the complete curriculum
for all princesses, including:

How to Talk to a Dragon

Creative Cooking for Perfect Palace Parties

Wishes, and How to Use Them Wisely

Designing and Creating the Perfect Ball Gown

Avoiding Magical Mistakes

Descending a Staircase as if Floating on Air

Our principal, Queen Gloriana, is present at all times, and students are in the excellent care of the school Fairy Godmother.

VISITING TUTORS AND EXPERTS INCLUDE:

KING PERCIVAL *(Dragons)*

LADY VICTORIA *(Banquets)*

QUEEN MOTHER MATILDA *(Etiquette, Posture, and Poise)*

THE GRAND HIGH DUCHESS DELIA *(Fashion)*

We award tiara points to encourage
our princesses toward the next level.
Each princess who earns enough points
in her first year is welcomed to the
Tiara Club and presented with a silver tiara.

Tiara Club princesses are invited to return
next year to Silver Towers, our very special
residence for Perfect Princesses, where they
may continue their education at a higher level.

PLEASE NOTE:

Princesses are expected to arrive
at the Academy with a *minimum* of:

TWENTY BALL GOWNS
*(with all necessary hoops,
petticoats, etc.)*

TWELVE DAY-DRESSES

SEVEN GOWNS
*suitable for garden parties
and other special daytime
occasions*

TWELVE TIARAS

DANCING SHOES
five pairs

VELVET SLIPPERS
three pairs

RIDING BOOTS
two pairs

*Cloaks, muffs, stoles, gloves,
and other essential
accessories, as required*

Hi! I'm Charlotte. Princess Charlotte. I'm very pleased to meet you, and I'm so glad you're going to keep me company at the Princess Academy. It's a very special school for special princesses, and I don't know how Princess Perfecta or Princess Floreen got in! But you? You're exactly right! So . . . Welcome to the academy!

I've been wondering if you've ever had one of those days when everything goes wrong. You have? Well, my very first day at the Princess Academy was just like that . . .

Chapter One

I stood in the doorway and stared. I'd never seen a school dormitory before, and I couldn't believe my eyes. It was a long, thin room, and although the walls were a lovely rose-pink, it was so empty. Just six dressers, six chairs, and six beds arranged in neat and tidy rows.

And a thought hit me—*zonk!*

I was going to have to SHARE with five other princesses!

I gasped. I did my best to pretend it was a sort of cough, but it wasn't easy. And then I saw something else, and my mouth dropped open, and I really couldn't close it.

Not one of the beds had satin sheets! The sheets were plain white cotton but did look very clean. All the same—how could *any* princess be expected to sleep on plain cotton sheets?

"Now dear, unpack your things and make yourself at home." Queen Gloriana smiled at me as if everything was perfectly normal, and waved me toward the bed by the window.

"You're the first one here in Rose Room, but the other princesses will be arriving any minute. They're all lovely girls, and I'm sure you'll become great friends!" The principal waved again as she glided away, her long velvet skirts brushing the floor as she went.

"Thank you, Your Majesty," I said as politely as I could, but my heart was thumping. I

hurried to the window and looked out. I was just in time to see my father's golden coach glinting in the sunshine before it turned the corner of the driveway and disappeared.

If I hadn't heard someone coming up the stairs, I'd have cried my eyes out. I mean, what *was* this place?

I'd been reading up about The Royal Palace Academy for the Preparation of Perfect Princesses for ages. The brochure was full of pictures of sweeping staircases and the magical lake with swans floating on their own reflections. Best of all, there was the Princess Academy Annual Birthday Ball. It looked *fabulous*. Imagine the most wonderful ballroom ever, with a dark blue ceiling lit by millions of tiny sparkly stars, and lots and lots of the most beautiful princesses in the loveliest dresses twirling around and around the room. And it all happened on the very first evening of the new school year!

I'd been dreaming about the Birthday Ball. I could imagine every head turning as I drifted onto the dance floor. I'd decided that my dress would be soft pink with lots of swirly petticoats, and my tiara would be so sparkly that everyone would be completely dazzled. No one would *ever* notice my hair was a boring brown color and my nose wasn't exactly perfect—because if I was at the Princess Academy Birthday Ball, then I'd be beautiful too.

I nagged and nagged Mom and Dad until they said I could go to the Academy, and then I nagged a whole lot more until Mom agreed to let me have the dress I'd imagined. (It wasn't *exactly* right, but it was close.) I counted every single day until the beginning of the school year.

But as I stared miserably out of the window, I knew I'd made a *huge* mistake. Queen Gloriana was

scary. The school was too big. The
dormitory was awful. I didn't want
to share a room with anyone, let

alone five girls I'd never even met.

I decided I absolutely *had* to run away. At once.

"Hello," said a voice from the doorway. I turned, blinking hard so whoever it was wouldn't see I was nearly crying.

Chapter Two

You know how sometimes you see someone, and you just *know* you're going to be best friends? Well, it was like that when I saw Princess Alice. She's got such pretty eyes, and dark hair that sort of bubbles around her face, and the most wonderful smile. She was smiling as she came into the room.

"It's kind of awful, isn't it?" she said cheerfully. "My big sister was here last year, and she told me it was like prison! It's supposed to be good for us and make us grateful for what we've got at home."

She flung her suitcase on the bed next to mine. "Do you mind?" she asked. "I don't want to be next to someone I don't like."

I felt a sort of glow inside. "That's fine by me," I said.

Alice grinned. "Let's hope the others are okay. My sis had to room with a princess who was *so* untidy

the whole dormitory was always
getting minus tiara points. *And* she
snored!"

I couldn't help laughing, but I
didn't know what she meant.
"What are tiara points?"

"It's amazing!" Alice's eyes

sparkled. "When you get five hundred—if you ever do—you get to join the Tiara Club!" She beamed ecstatically. "I can't wait! There's a fantastically wonderful party to celebrate, and you're given a whole bunch of presents, and you get to move up to the second year! And then you're a senior, and you stay in the Silver Towers, and you

have such an incredible time."

"*Wow!*" I said. I was just about to ask what happened if you *didn't* get five hundred points when the door banged open and four more girls came bursting into the room. When they saw me and Alice, they stopped and stood up straight. The tallest, who was beautiful in a very pale blonde kind of way, gave us

the most amazing curtsey. She went right down to the floor—and she didn't wobble one bit.

"Good afternoon," she said, and her voice was very sweet and clear. "I'm Princess Sophia. These are my friends, the Princesses Katie, Emily, and Daisy."

"I'm Alice," Alice said. She curtsied back—and she didn't wobble either! I began to worry. Every time I tried to curtsey I fell over.

Princess Katie winked at me. She had dancing green eyes and red-gold hair that curled all over her head.

"Don't be put off by Sophia," she said. "She just can't help showing off. It's terribly boring for her, being so beautiful, but she's okay really. Who are you?"

"I'm Princess Charlotte," I said.

"I just got here."

Katie nodded. "Us too," she said, and she sat down on a bed with a most un-princessy *flump*. "Are you excited about the ball tonight? We are! What are you going to wear? Is your dress here? Can we see it?"

I shook my head. "I've only got my everyday dresses. My ball gowns are coming later in the luggage cart."

"Mine too," Alice chipped in. "Gran said there wasn't any room in the coach." She giggled. "She and Granpapa came with me, and they both insisted on wearing their coronation robes, and there was only enough room left for me and the *teeniest* suitcase."

Princess Emily laughed. I'd thought she was a serious kind of girl, but when she laughed her blue eyes twinkled.

"We all came in Sophia's coach. It's *enormous*! We rattled around inside it like peas in a great big golden pod, but it did mean we could pile tons of luggage on the roof . . ."

Her voice suddenly trailed away, and her face went very pale.

"What's the matter, Em?" asked Princess Daisy. She was the littlest of us, and she had long black hair and the biggest brown eyes you ever saw. She patted Emily's hand anxiously. "What happened?"

"The luggage!" Emily said. "I know the coachman brought in our cases from *inside* the coach, but I'm almost sure he didn't get anything from the *outside*!"

There was a terrible silence. Then Sophia said, "Are you *really* sure, Emily?"

Katie dashed to the window and peered out.

"I can see our suitcases piled up by the steps," she said.

"And the trunks?" Emily asked,

her voice trembling. "Oh, *do* say they're there!"

Katie leaned out so far, I was scared she'd fall, but she didn't. She

pulled herself back in, her eyes shining.

"Quick!" she said. "The coach is still there—the coachman's talking to the footman by the front door! *And the trunks are on the roof!"*

Chapter Three

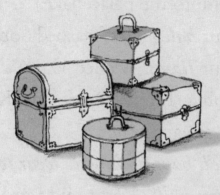

We all ran as fast as we could down the stairs—even the elegant Sophia. Surprised heads popped out from doors as we dashed past, but we didn't pay any attention to them. We poured out of the grand front door just in time to see an ancient coach rumbling away. It was headed toward the bridge over the river that flowed into the palace lake.

"Our *ball gowns*!" gasped Sophia.

"Our *tiaras*!" wailed Daisy.

Sophia, Emily, Daisy, and Katie stared at each other.

"We'll have nothing to wear to the birthday ball!" Katie said, and the other three burst into floods of tears.

Now, I'm truly not trying to brag, but I can run really fast. When I saw how upset Sophia, Katie, Emily, and Daisy were, I hitched up my skirts and I sprinted after that coach, yelling, *"Stop! Stop! Please stop!"*

I caught up with the coach just as it trundled onto the bridge. I could see the coachman had finally heard me because he turned around to look.

"Come back!" I shrieked.

I know it wasn't a princessy thing to do, but I *had* to make him stop. He pulled hard on the reins and the coach swung wildly. It was then that I saw the luggage cart lumbering up from the other side of the bridge . . .

The *crash* was terrible. The coach swayed, the cart tipped, and then every single trunk and suitcase fell into the river with a humongous *splash*!

I stood and stared, so shocked I

could hardly breathe.

Alice, Katie, Emily, Daisy, and Sophia suddenly appeared beside me, and they stared too. Only bubbles showed where our trunks had landed in the water.

And then an ice-cold voice spoke from behind us.

"Princess Charlotte, please come to my study *at once*. Princesses Alice, Daisy, Emily, Katie, and Sophia, I would like you to go back to your dormitory. *Now!*"

Queen Gloriana sounded so angry, my stomach felt as if it was tied into knots.

"Yes, Your Majesty," I whispered.

I tried to curtsey, and of course I wobbled so badly I had to clutch at Alice to stop myself from falling over.

I wanted to die.

I really, really did—especially when Queen Gloriana gave me a look of utter despisement, turned on her heel, and turned away toward the palace.

Alice slipped her hand into mine. "Oh, Charlotte," she said. "It was an accident."

I began to cry. I couldn't help it.

Katie took my other hand.

"We'll come with you," she said.

"We all will," said Sophia. "It

was *our* trunks you were trying to save."

Emily gave me a tissue, and Daisy looked at me solemnly.

"You were very brave," she said. "I could never have run like that."

They were all so nice, I felt a little bit better. And when we got to the principal's study, they insisted on coming in with me. I mumbled my way through a huge apology, and then Sophia explained about the coach riding away and me trying to stop it, and somehow she made it sound as if I'd almost been a hero.

Queen Gloriana listened without

saying a word. She has one of those very calm, regal sort of faces, and although she obviously thought I'd

been very foolish, she never said so. When Sophia had finished, the principal folded her hands on her desk and looked hard at me.

"It seems, Charlotte," she said, "that you are fortunate in your friends. And I believe that your heart is in the right place, even if you are too quick to act before you think. By now, the luggage should have been rescued from the water, and I have asked the pages to take your ball gowns to the Matron's room. If you can persuade Matron, or Fairy G. as we call her, to help you, then you may attend this evening's Birthday Ball. If, however, Fairy G. decides you are *not* worthy, then you will be excluded, together with your five friends.

"In addition, you will lose fifty tiara points, which will be a very poor beginning to your time here. I feel, Charlotte, that this will teach you a lesson you are unlikely to forget. And now you may go."

We shuffled outside in silence. I can't tell you how awful I felt. It was bad enough to get minus tiara points on my very first day at the Princess Academy, but the other punishment was the worst in the whole wide world.

We were going to miss the birthday ball . . . and it was all my fault!

Chapter Four

$\mathcal{A}$s we walked down the corridor, we passed a group of princesses looking at a bulletin board. As we got closer, they started whispering to each other, and a princess with a pointy nose said, "*Those* are the girls I was telling you about. They're in *big* trouble! They've got minus tiara points *already*!"

And the others sniggered.

Princess Sophia was wonderful. She swept past them with such a superior look on her face I almost laughed out loud.

"Ignore them!" she ordered, in her clear cool voice. "Princesses should support each other at all times—especially when things go wrong!" And she sailed on as if she hadn't a care in the world.

"That was Princess Floreen by the board," Alice said in my ear. "And Princess Perfecta was the one with the snooty stare. She was here last year, but she didn't earn enough points to join the Tiara Club, so she's back here again in the first year with us. My big sis says she's *ghastly*."

Princess Academy Notices

Curtseying Class on thursday

Princess Birthday Ball tonight!

Learn to float down stairs like a Princess

Pet frog

Creative Cookery after school

SPELLS CLUB! on tuesday

"Oh," I said, and then I noticed something. Emily and Daisy were both blowing their noses really really hard, and I instantly knew they were trying not to cry. I made up my mind. I *had* to convince Fairy G. that my new friends should be able to go to the Birthday Ball, even if I couldn't. Maybe—my stomach felt very wobbly at the thought—she could give me more minus tiara points instead.

Alice knew the way to the Matron's room, and we soon found ourselves outside a big door with a sign outside that said:

> ### ✦ FAIRY GODMOTHER ✦
> **Matron at the Princess Academy**
> **No frogs, toads, or spiders, if you please.**
> **P.S. No headache pills will**
> **be given to dragons.**

I took a deep breath and knocked.

"Come in!" boomed a loud and echoing voice. I nervously opened the door and peeped inside.

Fairy G. had an enormous red face and hair that stuck out in all directions, and she was dressed in a collection of shawls and scarves and floaty, drapey things. Behind her in a fireplace, a huge fire crackled and spat, and flames roared up the chimney.

All around the room were cabinets and shelves of bottles and jars and jugs, and strange-looking bunches of what might have been herbs. The biggest tabby cat I'd ever seen was curled up on the back of a giant armchair. It was all very weird—and a little bit scary.

And then I saw our ball gowns. They were hung over a long rack. I'd never seen anything so terrible. They were covered in weeds and mud, and were dripping all over the carpet. The fur was bedraggled, and there was a long loop of dull yellowing stars draped over a heap of dirty petticoats.

Sophia let out a little cry. The others gasped.

Worst of all, Alice let go of my

hand and clutched at Katie's arm.

"My beautiful dress!" she moaned. "Oh, look at it!"

"So," Fairy G. bellowed, looking straight at me, "you're the one who caused all of this. What have you got to say for yourself?"

I swallowed hard.

"It was my fault," I whispered. "I just didn't think. I ran after the coach—and the driver crashed because he was looking back at me. . . ."

And that was the exact moment

when a huge spark flew out of the fire. It landed on the thick carpet, and bright red-and-yellow flames shot up into the air.

Chapter Five

Everyone screamed. Daisy ran for the door. I could feel my jaw dropping, but I knew what I had to do. I snatched my sopping wet dress from the rack, flung it over the flames, and stamped on it.

There was a nasty smell of

burning silk, but the fire was out. I leaned against the wall, panting.

Then I saw that Fairy G. was *laughing*!

"Well done, Princess," she said, and her voice was softer now. She turned to the others. "You see, there *are* times when acting fast can save the day. And now that Princess Charlotte has saved my carpet, I think she deserves a wish. What would you like, my dear?" And her big, red face suddenly looked amazingly friendly.

Of course I wished that Alice, Daisy, Emily, Katie, and Sophia could have their dresses back as good as new.

"Excellent." Fairy G. beamed and snapped her big, fat fingers.

Have you ever seen sparkly pink fairy dust? Well, it's *amazing*. It floats in the air, smells like strawberries, gets up your nose in the nicest possible way, and makes you sneeze! And when we'd all stopped sneezing, there was the rack full of beautiful, beautiful, *beautiful* dresses on satin hangers, all looking even better than brand-new.

And a row of sparkling tiaras was balanced on the top.

"*Oooooooooooooooh!*" cried Daisy.

"Wow!" Katie and Emily said together. "Wow!"

"They're *wonderful*!" Sophia sighed.

Alice tucked her hand into mine. "Thanks!" she said. Her eyes were starry. "You're a *real* friend."

"Thank you so much, Fairy G.!" I said. I was feeling so happy, I was practically floating.

And then I saw my own wet, burned-black dress still lying in a soggy puddle on the carpet. My stomach was tied into knots, but I took a deep breath.

After all, it was my own fault. Maybe my special new friends would tell me about the Birthday Ball later, but I had to fight an enormous lump in my throat before I could speak.

"I'll take this away," I said, and I bent down to pick the dress up.

Alice was beside me in a flash. "I've got another ball gown," she said. "Please say you'll wear it! *Please*!"

I looked at Fairy G., a little glimmer of hope flickering inside me. She looked back at me and stroked her chin thoughtfully.

"Please, Fairy Godmother, please allow Charlotte to go to the ball!" Sophia gave Fairy G. one of her fantastic curtseys. Daisy, Emily, and Katie curtsied too. "Please," they echoed. *"Please!"*

"We wouldn't enjoy it without

Best friends forever!

her," Daisy added. "We're all best friends!"

"That's right!" Alice didn't curtsey, but she did a lovely twirl, her tiara held high in the air. "I hereby declare the Rose Room Girls best friends *forever*!"

I wanted to hug Alice when she said that. I'd always been the kind of girl who sticks to herself, and I'd been hoping to find some real friends at the Princess Academy—and now I knew I had! It was still my very first day, and I'd nearly ruined everything—but I was part of something really special. And I could see Katie's eyes were shining, and Sophia was smiling, and Emily and Daisy were nodding "yes" like mad.

Fairy G. began to chuckle. "Very well, then," she said. "All the members of the Rose Room shall go to the ball. But I think Princess

Charlotte had better wear her own dress, don't you?" And she took my dress from me.

More fairy dust twinkled in

the air . . . and there it was in my arms. It was so perfect, I couldn't believe my eyes. Soft pink, with swirly petticoats just like before, but now it was covered with sparkles of magical fairy dust. It was exactly what I'd always dreamed of.

"Just one more thing," Fairy G. said as she opened the door for us.

"There'll be no minus points for any of you. In fact—" her eyes began to twinkle "—I'll give each of you twenty *plus* tiara points! Twenty points each for true friendship."

We started to thank her, but she

waved us away. "Quick, quick, quick! Some of us have to get ready for the ball!" And she shooed us out.

As we went, I noticed that her carpet was perfect again. Not the smallest sign of a burn.

Fairy G. saw me looking and she winked as she shut the door firmly behind me.

Chapter Six

The Birthday Ball was utterly fantastic. Did I tell you that the ceiling of the ballroom was the most beautiful midnight blue—and full of twinkling stars? Well, something *amazing* happened there.

All of the new girls were asked to come in last. Fairy G. said it was a school tradition. We made sure the Rose Roomers all stayed together. We were the last to go in . . . and we were really *really* nervous. As we swept our way through the golden doors and into the ballroom (would you believe not one of us fell over?), Queen Gloriana was standing by her glittery throne waiting to greet us. We each sank into the deepest curtsey we could manage (even mine was okay). She smiled and said, "Welcome to the Princess Academy, my dears."

And then she nodded at Fairy G.,

who was standing next to her. Fairy G. waved her wand—and six new stars popped out of the dark blue sky and shone and sparkled . . . and if this sounds like I'm bragging, I'm really sorry, but *our stars were the biggest and twinkliest of them all!*

Then the music floated us away,

and around and around in our fabulous ball gowns (would you believe we were *all* wearing pink?), and we danced nonstop until the clock chimed midnight.

It was wonderful. And Alice,

Daisy, Emily, Katie, Sophia, and I chatted and giggled and laughed together all evening, and we had the very *very* best time.

Fairy G. came stomping up the dormitory stairs late that night to make sure we'd put the light out.

"Good night, Rose Room," she bellowed as she thundered away down the stairs.

And we all snuggled down in our cool white sheets, and I thought how lucky I was to be at the Princess Academy. I made myself a secret promise. I'd try my *very* best to be a member of the Tiara Club one day, with all my friends—especially you.

What happens next?

FIND OUT IN

✦ Princess Katie ✦
∽ AND THE ∽
Silver Pony

How do you do? It's great to meet you. We're all so glad you're here! Oh! Maybe you don't know who we are. We're the Princesses Katie (that's me), Charlotte, Emily, Alice, Daisy, and Sophia, and we share the Rose Room at the Princess Academy, and one day we'll all be members of the totally fabulous Tiara Club! Just as long as we get enough tiara points, of course.

Do you ever feel really tired after a party? Well, we had a wonderful time at the Birthday Ball here at the Academy, but for the next few days it was so hard to get up. . . .

You are cordially invited to visit www.tiaraclubbooks.com!

Visit your special princess friends at their dazzling website!

Find the secret word hidden in each of the first six Tiara Club books. Then go to the Tiara Club website, enter the secret word, and get an exclusive poster. Print out the poster for each book and save it. When you have all six, put them together to make one amazing poster of the entire Royal Princess Academy. Use the stickers in the books to decorate and make your very own perfect princess academy poster.

More fun at www.tiaraclubbooks.com:

- Download your own Tiara Club membership card!

- Win future Tiara Club books.

- Get activities and coloring sheets with every new book.

- Stay up-to-date with the princesses in this great series!

Visit www.tiaraclubbooks.com and be a part of the Tiara Club!